Sun Racers

Heather Hammonds

Chapter 1	**Solar Cars**	2
Chapter 2	**How Solar Cars Work**	4
Chapter 3	**Solar Car Races**	6
Chapter 4	**Solar Car Teams**	8
Chapter 5	**Before the Race**	12
Chapter 6	**The Race Begins**	14
Chapter 7	**Solar Bicycles**	18
Chapter 8	**What Is Learned**	20
Chapter 9	**Future Cars**	22
Glossary and Index		24

Chapter 1
Solar Cars

These cars look very different to most cars. They are called solar cars. Solar cars do not use **petrol** as **fuel**. They use energy from the sun to make them work.

These solar cars are racing cars. They race against other solar cars. They travel long distances and go very fast.

'Solar' means of or to do with the sun.

Chapter 2
How Solar Cars Work

Solar cars have lots of small **solar cells** on them. These solar cells turn sunlight into electricity. The electricity is used to make the solar cars work.

solar cells

Most solar cars need more than 1000 solar cells to make them go fast.

Solar cars have special shapes. This helps their solar cells get lots of sunlight. The special shapes also help solar cars go faster and use less electricity.

**Some solar cars have three wheels.
Other solar cars have four wheels.**

Chapter 3
Solar Car Races

Solar car races are held in different countries around the world. Race teams bring their solar cars to these races.

Some solar car races are called 'challenges'. They are very hard to win.

solar cars at the American Solar Challenge race

The first solar car races were held in the 1980s.

Most solar car races are held over several days.

Solar cars travel through deserts, over mountains and through towns.

They go on the same roads as other cars and trucks. They travel for thousands of kilometres.

Chapter 4
Solar Car Teams

A team of people work together to build and race a solar car.

It takes several months for each solar car team to build their car. All the parts of the car must be bought. Then they must be put together. Everyone works very hard to build the car.

Some solar car teams have just a few people in them. Other teams have more than thirty people!

Solar car racing is a team sport.

After a solar car has been built, it is tested. The team sees how fast their car can go. They check that it is working properly.

Teams choose names for their cars, such as *Sunswift*, *Sunshark* or *Sun Challenger*.

Some members of the team drive the solar car. They will take turns to drive the car during races.

Other members of the team look after the solar car. They will fix it if it breaks during races.

The solar car team members travel with the car during races. Everyone works together to try to win!

Chapter 5
Before the Race

There are lots of rules in solar car races. Before the start of every solar car race, **race officials** check all the solar cars. They make sure that the cars do not have more solar cells than allowed.

Sometimes the solar cars are weighed, measured and photographed.

Solar cars are also driven around a racetrack before a solar car race begins.

Race officials check to make sure the cars are safe to drive on the road.

The fastest cars on the racetrack usually get to go first at the start of a solar race.

Chapter 6
The Race Begins

After all the cars have been checked, the race begins. The solar cars drive away as their teams cheer them on. Big crowds come to see them go. The start of a solar car race is very exciting!

Solar car drivers drive as fast as they can along the roads. Some solar car team members travel ahead of their solar cars. They make sure the road is safe.

Other solar car team members travel behind their solar cars. Drivers talk to their teams on radios.

Solar cars must stop each night during solar car races.

Sometimes, solar cars break down during a race.

Solar car teams carry **spare parts** and tools with them to fix their cars. They work quickly, so the drivers can keep going in the race.

Solar car teams are very happy when their car reaches the end of a race. They have worked very hard to build and race their cars. They feel very proud when their car crosses the finish line.

In some solar car races, the fastest solar cars finish the race several days before the slowest solar cars!

Chapter 7
Solar Bicycles

Some bicycles also use energy from the sun to make them go. Solar bikes have pedals, just like normal bikes. They also have solar cells. The solar cells make electricity. The electricity is used to help the solar bikes go faster.

solar cells

Solar bikes cannot travel as fast as solar cars.

solar cells

Solar bikes go in races too. Some solar bikes look just like normal bikes. Other solar bikes look like small solar cars.

Chapter 8
What Is Learned

Solar cars and solar car races help people learn about **solar energy**.

Many solar car teams visit schools with their cars. Students learn how these cars work.

a solar car at a car show

Solar cars help scientists learn how to build better solar cells.

Solar cars also help scientists learn how to build other types of cars that use less petrol.

Solar cells are also used in these machines.

Chapter 9
Future Cars

Today's solar cars are very expensive. People do not drive them to work or school. The solar cars are built just to go in solar car races. Only one or two people can travel in these solar cars.

Every year, better, faster solar cars are built.

In the future, lots of cars might use energy from the sun to make them go. Perhaps one day, you will own a solar car!

Glossary

fuel   material that, when burned, makes energy to power machines and lights

petrol   a kind of fuel that can be used to make the motors of machines such as cars, buses and trucks go

race officials   the people in charge of a race that make sure everyone obeys the rules

solar cells   small machines that use energy from the sun to make electricity

solar energy   energy from the sun

spare parts   extra parts that can be used to build a machine such as a solar car

team sport   a sport that groups of people play, such as football or solar car racing

Index

building solar cars 8–9

race teams 4, 9–11, 14–17, 19

solar bikes 18–19

solar car drivers 10, 15–16

solar car races 3–5, 8–17, 19–20, 22

solar cells 6–7, 12, 18